A
TIGER
Tale

Look out for more books by Holly Webb

A Cat Called Penguin
The Chocolate Dog
Looking for Bear

For younger readers:

Magic Molly

1. The Witch's Kitten
2. The Wish Puppy
3. The Invisible Bunny
4. The Secret Pony
5. The Shy Piglet
6. The Good Luck Duck

For slightly older readers:

The Animal Magic stories

1. Catmagic
2. Dogmagic
3. Hamstermagic
4. Rabbitmagic
5. Birdmagic
6. Ponymagic
7. Mousemagic

www.holly-webb.com

A TIGER Tale

HOLLY WEBB
Illustrated by Catherine Rayner

■SCHOLASTIC

First published in the UK in 2014 by Scholastic Children's Books
An imprint of Scholastic Ltd
Euston House, 24 Eversholt Street
London, NW1 1DB, UK
Registered office: Westfield Road, Southam, Warwickshire, CV47 0RA
SCHOLASTIC and associated logos are trademarks and/
or registered trademarks of Scholastic Inc.

ISBN 978 1407 13863 3

A CIP catalogue record for this work is
available from the British Library.

Printed and bound by CPI Group (UK) Ltd, Croydon, CR0 4YY
Papers used by Scholastic Children's Books are made
from wood grown in sustainable forests.

1 3 5 7 9 10 8 6 4 2

www.scholastic.co.uk
www.holly-webb.com

For Annelie

And Harvey,

her gorgeous, stripy, tigerish cat

"I just keep thinking about him." Kate's mum smiled. "The stupidest things. Like him always complaining that the tea wasn't strong enough."

Auntie Lyn let out a snort of laughter. "Dad only drank tea if it was strong enough to take the paint off the mugs. Who knows what it did to his insides? He must have had a cast-iron stomach."

Kate listened to them talking over her head, and blinked worriedly. Was that what had happened? All those mugs of tea had done something awful to Granddad's stomach? But

Mum and Auntie Lyn were laughing, so it couldn't be true.

She wanted to join in – to say that Granddad was brilliant at dunking biscuits, and his biscuits never fell apart in his tea, ever. He let Kate dunk

them too, but she always whipped them out again after a couple of seconds, just in case they crumbled. And actually because she didn't really like the taste of tea. She only did it because Granddad did.

She wanted to say it, but somehow the words wouldn't come out of her mouth. She just stayed sitting silently on the sofa, between Mum and Auntie Lyn, listening.

All those stories. Her dad was telling them too, and Mrs Eversley, Granddad's friend from down the road. And a couple of other people – relatives who'd come for the funeral. Mum had told Kate who they were, but there were so many people around, and she just couldn't remember. They'd all known Granddad, and everyone seemed to have something to say.

Granddad wearing odd shoes to the supermarket. Granddad flying a kite with Kate in the park – everyone looked at her when Dad said that, but Kate still couldn't say anything. Granddad taking ages to walk down the street on sunny days, because he had to stop and say hello to all the sunbathing cats.

That made Kate smile. It was so true. He'd nearly made her and Molly late for school, a few weeks back. That black cat from the house on the corner had rolled on its back on the dusty pavement, and then followed them down the street. They'd had to stop and shoo it home, just in case it tried to cross the road.

Kate smiled, and then bit her bottom lip hard to make herself stop. She mustn't smile. Granddad was *dead*. How could she be happy?

She didn't understand how everyone could tell stories and laugh. Her words were building up inside her, all the things she wanted to say too, but couldn't. They hurt, deep inside her chest, much more than her bitten lip did.

Granddad had walked them to school every day, and usually he picked them up again too. That was making Kate feel even worse. What would happen after the Easter holidays, when they went back to school? Who would pick them up now? Kate sank her chin down under the neck of her best cardigan and tried not to cry any more. Her eyes were aching.

She supposed it was mean to be worrying about who was going to take them to school and back. It seemed selfish, but she couldn't help thinking about it. Granddad had always been there, and now he wasn't.

Until a week ago, he'd lived in the little flat that used to be the garage at the side of Kate's house. He'd been there for four years, half as long as Kate had been alive. And even before that he'd lived close by, in the house he'd shared with Kate's Gran, five minutes' walk away. Kate didn't remember Gran much at all, as she had died when Kate was only a baby. Granddad had been lonely living on his own, so he'd come to live with them. Now it felt to Kate as if he'd always been there.

Granddad had cooked tea sometimes too, if Mum and Dad had to work really late. He made brilliant cheese on toast. (Which was lucky, because it was all he ever made, that and toffee. But Kate didn't mind – they were two of her favourite things.)

The voices went on murmuring over her head, and still her stories were locked away inside her. Kate felt as though she couldn't stand it any longer. She wriggled out from between her mum and Auntie Lyn, and threaded her way through everyone's legs.

"Are you all right, Kate?" her mum asked, turning away from listening to Mrs Eversley for a moment.

"Mmm. Just going upstairs for a bit."

"Molly's upstairs too," her mum suggested. "You could go and sit with her."

Kate nodded, but she knew that she wouldn't. Molly's bedroom door would be tight shut, and if Kate interrupted her she'd probably get yelled at. She climbed the stairs wearily, wondering what to do. She was tired, but it was too early to go to bed – it was only about six o'clock. On a usual day, Mum and Dad would just be getting home from work. Kate would have been pottering around the garden with Granddad, or sitting at the kitchen table doing her homework, or drawing. She stopped on the top step of the stairs, sniffing.

Molly's door was shut, and there was a notice on it that said *Go Away*, in very large black letters. And underneath in smaller pink letters it said, *This means you*. There was no point even asking if she could be with her sister. But as Kate pushed her own bedroom door, just next to Molly's, she already knew she couldn't stay in there either. Her room was full of things that she ought to want to be doing, like her jewellery kit, and a book of disgusting science experiments. But Granddad had bought her that – he'd promised to help her with it. And her fingers felt too tired and sausage-like for threading beads today.

She jumped as Molly's bedroom door opened, very suddenly, and her sister glared out, red-eyed and grumpy. "What do you want? Why are you just standing there?"

"I'm not. . ." Kate said at once, even though she was. "I'm standing in my room. Go away." She took a small step further into her room, to make it true, and Molly sighed huffily and whisked back. Kate heard the bedsprings wheeze as Molly flung herself down.

Kate stood in the doorway, and sighed at her room. Usually she loved to curl up on the scruffy old armchair by the window. Even if she was in a bad mood, or she'd had a fight with Molly, the faded plush fabric and musty smell made her feel better. Today, it wasn't enough.

But there was a striped, droopy-whiskered

face squashed between the cushions. Kate picked up Amos, and hugged him tight. He was saggy, and his fur stuck up in odd spikes from being squashed under Kate's chin when she was asleep, but he still looked proud, and brave, and wise, like a real tiger.

It was silly, Kate thought, sniffing again, that Amos could make her feel so much better and so much worse *at the same time*. He always made her happy, because he was her favourite toy, her best and most special thing. But Amos had been a present from Granddad, two years' ago. He even looked like Granddad, a little bit, with the same fabulous furry eyebrows over his yellow marbley eyes. Grandad's eyes had peered out from under his eyebrows just like that, the last time she'd seen him. They'd been in the shed,

11

Granddad humming to himself and looking at his seed catalogues, and Kate sitting next to him writing. Another story about a brave, fierce princess, and her pet tiger. She had been writing it for months, in episodes, and with pictures too. Granddad had read Kate's story, and twitched his eyebrows at all the best bits.

She would go to the shed, Kate decided, brushing Amos's furry eyebrows against her cheek. She could even look at the seed catalogues. She loved them – the pictures of the flowers were nice enough, but the names were brilliant. Most of her characters' names had come out of Granddad's catalogues. Her princess was called Gloriosa (Glory for short), and the evil witch who kept trying to steal Amos was called Scabiosa. Scabiosa were actually quite pretty flowers, like fluffy little pom-poms. But they sounded wart-encrusted and witch-like.

"Where are you going?" Molly growled, as Kate passed her door again.

"Downstairs." It was true, even if she wasn't planning to stay there. . .

"Why've you got that ratty toy tiger? You're eight, not four. You're too big to be carrying toys around."

Kate stared back at Molly, wondering why she had to be so mean. Molly had toys as well – a whole shelf full of dolls that she swore she didn't ever play with, but she still wouldn't let Mum give them to the charity shop. And they weren't dusty, either, like things that never got touched. Kate knew that Molly brushed their hair, and held them – but only when she was sure no one could see her. Maybe when she was ten she wouldn't want Amos, Kate thought, and tears burned her eyes again. She didn't want to be that old. That *horrible*.

"You look like a baby," Molly snapped, propping herself up on her elbows and glaring at Kate. "Oh, stop crying! You ought to throw that stupid old thing away." She wriggled upright, reaching out as though she was going to snatch Amos, and Kate darted away with a frightened squeak.

"No!"

Kate ran down the stairs in a rush. She'd meant to creep down, step by step, to make sure Mum or Dad didn't hear her. She didn't want to explain why she was going outside. Kate had a feeling that Mum would say sitting in

14

Granddad's shed was silly – or wrong, somehow. She couldn't see why. It was just like telling stories about him, except that she wanted to be *in* the story instead, with all the things that reminded her of Granddad.

2

No one heard her, even though she'd forgotten to tiptoe. They were too busy talking. Kate hurried past the living-room door and into the kitchen. Then she peered out of the back door at the garden. It looked brighter than the house. Less miserable. And a lot less full of people that Kate had to be polite to.

The sun was low and golden, and Kate could smell the wallflowers that Granddad had planted along the path that wound through the garden. There were bees bumbling slowly in and out of them, and she loved the way they zigzagged about, as though nothing mattered but that honey-sweet smell. *Did bumblebees even look where they were going?* she wondered. What would happen if they crashed into each other? Bumblebees were practically all whisker and fluff, so perhaps they could feel each other coming. And even if they did crash, Kate thought, as she went on down the path, it would be like bumper cars. They'd just bounce off each other.

Granddad had told her that cats used their whiskers to measure if they could get through a hole without getting stuck. If their whiskers went through, he said, the rest of them would. Though they hadn't been sure if that would apply to Fat Ginger, the cat next-door-but-one. He had average-sized whiskers, but the rest of him was *enormous*. Even his tail was fat. But then

Molly had pointed out that she couldn't see Fat Ginger making the effort to try to get through a hole anyway, unless there was a great big bowl of food on the other side.

The shed door creaked as she opened it, and Kate looked up at the can of WD-40 on the shelf. Granddad put it on the hinges when they squeaked, and Kate always reminded him when it needed doing. Just for a second, she turned round to look up at him following her down the path, to see if he'd noticed. But he wasn't there, of course.

That was the point.

Kate gulped and swallowed a few times, trying to get past the strange feeling in her throat. Was it all right just to spray the stuff on the door herself? She had promised never to touch the tools or the bottles and jars in the shed without Granddad there to help. But everything had changed now. Mum and Dad wouldn't remember the squeaky door.

She didn't do it. She reached up for the can – touched it, even. It was dusty, and tacky with grease, and she could feel the cool liquid sloshing inside it. But then she put it back. Granddad hardly ever yelled, but he could be serious. If he'd seen her messing, his eyebrows would have met in the middle, the way they did when he was worried, or upset, or cross.

Kate pushed the can to the back of the shelf behind the cat treats, and rubbed her fingers clean on a tissue from her pocket. Mum had been handing them out all day.

Then she curled up on the dusty wooden

floor, next to the bench with all the flowerpots on it. There was a canvas chair in the shed for Granddad to sit in while he was looking at his seed catalogues, or sometimes just reading the newspaper, and looking out of the shed door at the garden. Granddad said it was the best view of the rose bushes, out of the door of the shed. But Kate always sat on the floor, even if Granddad wasn't there. Her pencils were on the bottom shelf of the potting bench, and her notebook.

She balanced Amos on the seat of the chair, looking down at her like Granddad did. But she didn't get out her notebook. She couldn't think of a story, at all. Even all the ideas she'd had before, the ones she'd been saving up, seemed to be stuck inside her. Just like the stories about Granddad. Everything was jumbled up and set in a thick, sticky mess in her head.

Kate leaned back, resting her head against the wall of the shed and looking over at Amos. His paws were hanging down over the edge of the chair, folded over each other. Great, fat, floppy, lounging paws, like a real tiger. He *was* a real tiger too, of course.

Somewhere in India, an enormous Amos was prowling around in the forest, or sprawled over a branch high up in a great tree. Granddad had bought Kate a bit of Amos for her birthday, two years ago, after they had seen a tiger at the zoo and Kate had cried. She cried partly because he was so lovely, and so furry and striped, and she wanted him – but also because he had looked so bored.

The tiger had been walking back and forth along the glass wall of his enclosure, as though he was trying to find a way out. It was a very good zoo, Granddad had explained. The cages were big – so big that you couldn't always see the animals if they didn't feel like it, which Kate could quite understand. Who would want to have a window in their bedroom, so people could stare in, even when you were sulking? But even with his carefully planted habitat, and his pool, and his tiny, pretty forest, Kate was sure the tiger was miserable.

So for Christmas, Granddad had bought her a wild tiger. They sent money for him to be looked after, and protected from poachers, and every few months Kate got a letter, with photos of Amos and the other tigers in the national park. Kate had loved her own soft Amos ever since she had unwrapped the paw-print paper Granddad had done him up in. And she didn't care if she was too old to cuddle him. Not much, anyway. . .

If the real Amos ever met Molly, he'd probably eat her.

It was quite warm in the shed – the low evening sun was shining through the little window, sending sun and shadow stripes across the grimy floor. One of the bumblebees had followed her down the garden, and now it was blundering in and out of the bars of sunlight, gently buzzing.

She had been right to come down here, Kate thought sleepily. It had been such an odd, miserable sort of day, and it seemed to have been going on for ages. Kate was so tired that even leaning against the wooden wall of the shed felt comfortable. She yawned and rubbed her sticky eyes. She had been awake so early, worrying about the funeral. Today was supposed to have been all about Granddad, but she hadn't felt like it was the Granddad she knew. Now she could almost imagine that he was standing next to her, humming to himself as he potted up seedlings. It was a good way to remember him.

The sunlit stripes shimmered and reformed, like the light flickering through branches on a forest floor. Kate blinked, and the bumblebee buzzed louder. It was almost roaring now, Kate thought, like a tiny aeroplane, or a . . . or a tiger. . .

He came slinking through the shadow patches and out behind the old deckchairs in the corner, huge and heavy-shouldered, his head hanging low.

Kate was too surprised to run, or scream, or do anything sensible. She just stared, as the enormous cat padded towards her on his great velvety paws. His eyes were like her cuddly Amos's eyes, Kate noticed – just the same yellowish colour. But this was a real tiger, and the eyes shone like golden lamps in the dim evening light of the shed.

The tiger stood over her for a moment, and Kate wondered if he was hungry. She didn't have anything a tiger might like to eat. Only a few cat treats. Not even a tin of cat food. He could probably eat that with the tin still on, she thought, shivering a little as he yawned, and showed his teeth and the bright pinkness of his tongue. Or perhaps he'd prefer to eat her.

But the tiger simply nudged Kate out of the way, squashing her into the corner of the potting bench. Then he slumped down beside her with a thump that shook the shed. He looked at her, curled up against the wall, and bumped her with his nose, the way the cats in the street did. His nose was just like a cat's too, she noticed – apricot-pink and the same shape, with a sprawling fan of white whiskers.

His nose was damp and soft when he brushed against her cheek. Kate closed her eyes, and then opened them again, expecting that the tiger would have disappeared. There couldn't *actually* be a tiger in her shed. But he was still there, gazing at her expectantly – and purring. A deep, throaty sort of purr. Like Fat Ginger, only about a hundred times bigger.

All the information she'd had from the tiger charity had said how fierce and dangerous they were. How the keepers in the parks had to dart them with sleeping drugs if they wanted to do medical checks on them – there was no way the tigers would let people come close. Except that this one was snuggling up next to her like a pet cat. Maybe he was a trained tiger, from a circus, or something like that, Kate thought, cautiously lifting her hand to stroke his muzzle, even though she knew it was stupid. He could bite her hand off. But he had hair sticking out of his ears, like Granddad did. . . Kate reached out her fingers, and closed her eyes.

The tiger ducked his head helpfully, and let out a low, contented rumble. He liked it. Kate was stroking a tiger's ears, and the tiger was purring. . .

He nudged at her again, and bumped her with one fat paw – the dagger claws safely tucked away. He wanted her out of the corner, Kate realized. She scooted forward, and the tiger wrapped himself around her, as if she were a cub.

He was definitely a most unusual tiger, Kate told herself dreamily. Tigers weren't usually good fathers at all. They hardly ever saw their cubs, and left the tiger mothers to do all the work. But this tiger was fussing over her, nuzzling her so she lay curled up against his huge shoulder. Then he yawned. His front teeth were so huge they almost looked like knives, Kate thought, lying pillowed against his side. But when he closed his jaws again, and laid his massive head down on his paws and purred, she could almost swear he was a house cat. Only a big one.

She could feel his purrs rumbling through her, as she fell asleep.

3

Kate stirred as the tiger shifted next to her. She blinked, confused. The shed was dark now, except for a thin beam of light dancing on the floor.

"There you are!" Her dad's voice was full of relief as the torchlight found her face. "We didn't know where you'd gone, Kate."

Even in the darkness of the shed, Kate could see him gazing down at her worriedly. Of course he was worried. She would be too, if she'd just walked in.

"It's all right," she murmured sleepily, about to explain that the tiger wasn't fierce. And then she realized that the tiger wasn't there. He had gone, and she was curled on the floor of the shed, alone except for the toy Amos tucked under her arm.

"Come on, sweetheart." Dad crouched down and lifted her up. "You must be freezing. Let's get you up to bed."

"But the tiger. . ." Kate started to murmur. Then she stopped. Perhaps it had all been a dream. There was a sudden burning behind her eyes as she realized that of course it must have been. How could she have been so stupid? She'd fallen asleep – Dad had just woken her up, so she must have slept. She had only dreamed the tiger, even though it had seemed so real. And she had so wanted him to be real. Only something so amazing, so special, so strange, had made her stop wanting to cry and cry until Granddad came back.

"What did you say?" Dad asked gently. "I think you're still half asleep." He stood up, cradling Kate against his shoulder, and walked her out of the shed and back to the house.

Kate blinked at the brightness of the kitchen light, and buried her face in her dad's jumper. She didn't want to look at anyone, or talk to anyone. Not even her mum.

It was as Mum was helping her find her pyjamas that Kate noticed the hairs. All over her best cardigan. Soft, gingery-brown hairs, like tiger fur.

Kate sat in the back of the car, looking at the building, and the bright signs outside. She'd never been to anything like this before. And she didn't want to start now.

Mum and Molly were already on the pavement, and Mum opened her door. "We need to go, Kate. Come on." She didn't sound cross – more worried. But Kate could tell that she was jittering inside, knowing she needed to get to work. She wanted Kate and Molly nice and tidily out of the way.

Maybe that wasn't totally fair, Kate admitted to herself. But it felt true. Like they were being put away in a neat little box until Mum had time to deal with them again.

They'd explained it all yesterday, the day after Granddad's funeral. Mum was obviously trying to do her best to cheer them both up – she insisted that they all sat down and watched a film together, and she even made popcorn, properly in a pan. She made a big fuss over it, but the good mood didn't last long. That was when Mum said that both she and Dad had to go back to work on Monday, even though it was still the Easter holidays. They'd had time off while Granddad was in hospital, and to organize the funeral. But now that was over, and things had to go back to normal.

Kate had stared at Mum when she said that. Normal? Normal was Granddad being there and looking after them in the holidays, with Mum or Dad taking days off here and there so they could do special things together. *Normal* wasn't ever going to happen again.

Mum had backtracked, trying to explain that this new way of doing things might be difficult at first, but they'd all get used to it. But as far as Kate could see, the new way just meant other people looking after her. People she didn't like. People she didn't even *know*.

The holiday club wasn't even that close to home. No one from her school was going to be there. Her best friend Rosie went to one that was at their school, and Kate thought that would probably have been OK. At least she'd know where everything was, and lots of the classroom assistants from school worked in the holiday club too. Rosie said it was fun, getting to go in the other classrooms and nose about a bit. But that holiday club had been booked up weeks before.

So now she was stuck here, with no one she knew, except for Molly, and right now Kate would have much preferred it if Molly was somewhere else. Her sister was still being horrible, all the time. It was as if she couldn't see Kate without having to think of something nasty to say to her. And no one was even telling her off about it.

"It's only for a week, Katey-kitten," Mum said gently. But even Granddad's old pet name didn't make Kate feel any better. Especially not with Molly rolling her eyes and making sick-faces in the background. And it wasn't just for a week. It would be all the other holidays too. Mum and Dad hadn't worked out what was going to happen when they went back to school either. Who would drop them off and pick them up? Kate and Molly might have to go to a childminder, they said.

Kate thought that sounded terrible. A total stranger's house, after school, every day?

But actually, she wouldn't mind where they

went, if only they could go home afterwards, and it would be proper home again, with Granddad there.

She followed her mum inside, her arms wrapped tightly round her rucksack. Her lunch was in there, and her coat, but most importantly, she had Amos buried at the bottom. She didn't usually bring a toy out with her for the day – she'd never take Amos to school. But today, she felt like she needed him. He'd been on her bed as she got ready, and she'd snatched him up and stuffed him into the rucksack. She needed *somebody*.

"This looks lovely," Kate's mum whispered, nudging her, and smiling hopefully. "Look at the programme, Kate. Drama. Dance sessions. Look, pond-dipping, even! You'll have such a good time."

Molly had been looking almost as gloomy as Kate, but then she suddenly brightened as she saw a girl she knew from her year at school. Kate recognized her too, but she didn't know any of the other people milling around by the coat hooks. She stood there clutching her bag, watching as Molly walked off chatting with Erin, and feeling more alone than ever. A minute ago she'd wanted Molly to be somewhere else, and now she was, and Kate felt lost without her.

A chirpy, bouncy-looking girl in a staff T-shirt came over to her, smiling, and Kate shrank back against her mum. She didn't want to be persuaded into joining in with things, as this girl obviously intended. She just wanted to be left alone.

"Hi Kate!"

Was it her imagination, or did the girl – Jasmine, her badge said – did Jasmine have that note in her voice? The "I must be extra-sympathetic to this poor little girl because her granddad is dead" voice that some of the people at the funeral had used. It made Kate want to bite.

"What would you like to do first?" Jasmine asked cheerfully. "Your mum said you were great at art when she signed you up. We've got a huge poster wall in one of the classrooms, and we want to fill it all up by the end of the week. How about that?"

Kate glanced round hopelessly at her mum, but she was looking at her watch, wrinkling her nose worriedly. She was late.

Kate turned back to Jasmine and bared her

teeth in an unconvincing smile. "That would be nice," she said, in a voice that made it clear that she couldn't think of anything worse, and she would be ducking out of all the organized *fun* as soon as she possibly could.

If Kate hadn't been so sad, and so angry with Mum and Dad (and even Granddad) for dumping her here, she would have enjoyed the holiday club. The art room was full of huge, clean pieces of paper, and the sorts of things that Kate usually loved. Metallic crayons. Thick acrylic paint in fabulous colours. Bits of fabric cut up for collages. There was even someone there with different crafts to try out. She'd almost given in when she saw them laying out the stuff for making pâpier maché.

But instead she sneaked away, and hid herself in the loos for a bit, until everyone thought she was somewhere else. Then she hurried back to the coat hooks, and sat down on the floor with her rucksack in her lap. She didn't even need to get Amos out. She knew he was there.

She reached a hand in under her lunch box, and the anxious, out-of-breath nervous feeling lifted a little bit as she felt Amos's soft fur. It was silky, and cool – not like the warm roughness of the real tiger's fur. She remembered it, from that night after the funeral. Tiger fur looked soft in pictures, but it was coarse and thick, even a little scratchy. A tiger had been there, on Saturday night. He was real. He had left hairs on her cardigan. It was only that he'd had to go before Dad came and saw him. But she was almost sure he would come back. Granddad had given her Amos because he knew how much Kate loved tigers. It couldn't just be an accident that now Granddad was gone, a real tiger had appeared. Granddad had sent him. The tiger was there to look after her instead.

She unzipped her rucksack and peered at Amos's face, squashed down at the bottom of the bag. His glassy golden eyes gleamed. The tiger in the shed had golden eyes too, pale orangey-gold. Just like Amos. "Was it you?" Kate whispered, and Amos stared back at her calmly. Had he come alive? It sounded silly. But where else could the tiger have come from? She could almost hear his heavy, rumbling purr. It would be all right. *She* would be all right, as long as she had him with her. Her tiger would look after her.

A door opened somewhere down the passageway, and Kate hung her bag back up hurriedly and darted in through the nearest door. The library. It was empty, but no one had said they couldn't be in here.

There were footsteps following her down the passage, so she curled up under a table, and sat silent. She could wait, and watch, like a quiet tiger, and when the door opened, she simply curled herself away even tighter, and closed her eyes.

It was easier than she'd expected it to be. She sat there daydreaming about tigers – her special tiger and the adventures they could have together. It was as if she went away somewhere else, and no one knew. Her and Granddad and Amos, the real Amos, padding through the jungle. Granddad had a flask of tea, and the old sun hat he wore in the garden sometimes. They had gone hunting and she was lying next to her tiger on a broad tree branch, watching a deer padding by beneath them, when someone poked her.

Kate jumped, hitting her head on the table, and glared back at the girls staring in at her.

"What do you want?" she said, her eyes watering. Her head really hurt.

"Are you Kate? You aren't supposed to be under there. People are looking for you," one of the girls said.

"And it's lunchtime," the other one added. "What are you doing under there? Are you crying?"

"No," Kate muttered, wriggling out,

and hurrying past them to the door. She could hear them giggling behind her, and whispering about her. But she didn't care. Or at least, she tried not to.

"She was really embarrassing!" Molly hissed, glaring at Kate from the front seat. "People were talking about her. She wouldn't talk to anybody, and then she got lost, or something. Everyone was asking me if that was my sister."

"You could have said no," Kate muttered. She was sitting behind Molly, with her arms wrapped round Amos.

"What happened, Kate?" her mum asked worriedly. "They didn't say you got lost. Just that you were a bit shy."

"I wasn't lost, I was in the library. Reading. I didn't know I wasn't supposed to be there. Nobody *said*."

"Nobody else was weird enough to go off on their own!" Molly snapped.

Kate stared out of the window, biting at her lip to stop herself crying again. She was tired of crying. She didn't want to be miserable like this, but how was she supposed to make it stop? She couldn't cheer up all by herself. And everyone thought she was weird, so they were avoiding her. It was as if nobody liked her any more. Not even her own sister.

4

"Kate."

Kate jumped. She was lying on her bed, with Amos tucked underneath her, hoping to feel him purring again. She didn't know how to turn him real, how to make the tiger appear, but after her miserable day, she needed him to be huge again. She knew if she curled up in his paws, like she had in the shed, she would feel better.

"Sorry. I didn't mean to scare you." Her mum came in and sat down next to her on the bed. "I wanted to talk to you."

"I said I'm sorry! I didn't mean for them to lose me!" Kate had her fingers crossed down the side of the bed, but Mum didn't notice.

"It's not about that, Kate. Well. . . It is in a way. I'm not cross, I'm worried about you. I know you're sad about Granddad – we all are. But is there anything that would help? Anything that Dad or I could do to make you feel a bit less sad?"

Kate turned her face away. How could she feel better about Granddad not being there any more? It was a stupid question. The only thing that would make her feel better was if Granddad came back. Didn't they understand that?

"I don't want to talk about it," she muttered into her pillow.

Her mum sat there for a few moments, then she sighed, stroked her hand over Kate's hair and got up.

"Just say if you do. Please, love."

Kate waited until she'd heard Mum go back downstairs, and then she sat up, wrapping her arms round her knees.

It felt like she wasn't allowed to be sad any more. As though Mum and Dad and Molly wanted her to get over Granddad, and get on with things again, like they had. But Kate just didn't see how.

She slid off her bed, and went to peer round her door. Mum was in the kitchen, making dinner, so it would be tricky to go out to the shed again without explaining why. Which she really didn't want to do. But she could go and sit in Granddad's room instead. If her tiger wouldn't come, being in there would help her remember them both.

Granddad's bedroom had been the garage before, so it was downstairs. The door to it opened from the hallway, opposite the living room. Kate hung over the end of the stairs, watching out. Dad wasn't home yet, and Molly was watching TV in the living room. Mum was leaning over the hob, stirring something. Kate wasn't sure why she felt like she had to hide what she was doing. She hadn't gone into Granddad's room much before, but that was only because he wasn't usually in it. He was in the garden, or watching TV with her and Molly, or drinking tea in the kitchen. It wasn't that she wasn't allowed in there.

Kate pushed the door open, and stood just inside, looking round. Something invisible squeezed her stomach into a ball, and she felt suddenly sick.

It was all wrong. Someone – probably her mum – had tidied the whole room up. She'd taken the great pile of detective stories from next to Granddad's bed back to the library. She would have had to, Kate supposed, or they'd get late book fines, but it looked so strange seeing Granddad's bedside table with no books. His reading glasses were gone, and the glass where he put his teeth. The room smelled of washing powder. Mum had put new sheets on the bed, then. All of Granddad had been swept away.

Kate stumbled out, and into the kitchen, tucking Amos under her arm as she fumbled with the back door keys. She had to get to the shed, where everything was still the same.

"Are you going outside?" her mum asked,

looking surprised as she turned round from the pans.

Kate didn't answer. Of course she was!

"It'll be dark soon."

"I won't be long," Kate muttered, turning the key at last.

"Only ten minutes or so till dinner, Kate! Dad'll be home in a minute."

"All right." Kate banged the door behind her and raced down the path, gasping with relief when she saw that the shed looked exactly the same. Granddad was still almost there. He could have just put down his trowel and gone back to the house to put the kettle on.

His grubby old green fleece jacket was hanging up just inside the door. Kate pressed it against her cheek. The smell reminded her of Granddad – earth and rain and mint imperials. Granddad always laughed at her for running inside when it rained. He said she was a fragile little flower, and a bit of wet never hurt anybody.

Kate pulled the jacket off the hook and slipped it round her shoulders – it was chilly out in the shed, but the jacket made her feel warm all through, not just on the outside. But what if Mum came in and tidied up the shed? What if she washed Granddad's jacket, or gave it to a charity shop? Kate smiled to herself, just a little. A charity shop probably wouldn't want this jacket, she thought. It had holes in the cuffs, and it was all droopy and sagging. Mum had bought Granddad a new fleece for his last birthday, but Granddad had kissed her and said it was lovely, and then put it in the bottom of his wardrobe, and left it there. He'd told Kate it was too nice to wear. Besides, he was fond of the old one. It was worn in, he said. He'd just got it the way he liked it.

Kate picked up the pile of catalogues on Granddad's chair and opened the one on top. They were full of tiny bright pictures of flowers, and here and there a photo had been ringed in purple felt tip. One of her felt tips. She'd sat with Granddad at the kitchen table, drinking tea and eating biscuits (Kate had just had the biscuits) while they chose the bulbs for the garden this year. Kate had begged for red-and-white stripy tulips, because they were beautiful in the photo, and because she liked the name, Estella Rynveld. She was planning to add a mermaid called

Estella to her book. Granddad hadn't been convinced about the stripes (he liked something a bit less flashy, he said), but he'd given in. He'd chosen some apricot-coloured ones, so Kate had circled both, and then she'd helped him dig the holes, back in November. It had been raining, but Kate had stayed out anyway even though she could hardly feel her fingers. She felt responsible for those stripy Estellas.

She sat in the shed doorway and looked down the garden. She could see them, both lots, planted in clumps in the flower bed. Her stripy ones weren't out yet – they were just fat green buds. But Granddad's Apricot Beauties had opened over the last few days. On the day of the funeral Kate had noticed them out of her bedroom window. They were tall and strong, with flowers like perfect little cups. Even nicer than in the picture, Kate thought, looking down at the catalogue to see.

The purple felt-tip ring around the apricot tulips was seeping ink. She was crying again, without even noticing. Hurriedly she blotted the tear away with the hem of Granddad's fleece.

It seemed all wrong to Kate that she was here in the garden, and the flowers they'd chosen together were opening, but Granddad had gone. How could that be the way things were supposed to happen? It just wasn't fair.

She huddled Granddad's fleece around her and Amos, and watched the soft peachy-orange flowers shift in the wind. The fleece wrapped round Kate like soft, fat tiger paws, and deep tiger purrs rumbled in her ears. He'd come back!

The tiger nudged himself against her side, nuzzling against Granddad's old fleece, and Kate sighed shakily. "You're here. . ." she whispered. The tiger stayed behind her, gently rubbing against her arm. Kate didn't look round to see him properly. It was enough to know her tiger was there with her, keeping her safe for Granddad.

5

Kate sat in the corner of one of the classrooms, reading a book. She wasn't getting very far with it – it was a disguise, more than anything. Something she could say she was doing, if one of the staff tried to persuade her to join in an activity.

It wasn't a very interesting book, though. It was about mermaids, and it had looked quite good, but the story was so stupid that Kate was having trouble even pretending to read it. She wriggled herself deeper into the beanbag, and flicked over the next few pages in an unenthusiastic sort of way.

Ella and Izzy, the two girls who'd found her under the table the day before, were practising a dance routine on the other side of the classroom. Kate watched them, a little wistfully. She did ballet classes, and street dance, and she wished she could go and join in. Both Ella and Izzy were very good – even though they were dancing to music on Ella's MP3 player, and sharing the earphones, which didn't make it easy. They couldn't move more than about thirty centimetres away from each other.

The earphones shot out of Ella's ears as she kicked out too energetically, and she tried to catch them and practically fell over. Izzy tried to catch her, and the pair of them staggered all over the classroom, giggling, and nearly fell into Kate and her beanbag.

"Oooops! Sorry!" Izzy perched on the edge of the beanbag for a minute. "I think we twirled too much. I'm dizzy."

"You looked really good," Kate told her shyly. Molly had said everyone thought she was weird. Izzy might not want to talk to her.

"Do you think so?" Izzy sounded pleased. "We've been practising it for a while. But really it needs more people." She glanced sideways at Ella, who stared at Kate thoughtfully and jerked her head in a tiny nod.

"Do you want to be in it too?" Izzy suggested. "We could sing the music – we've not got any more earphones." She stood up, and held out a hand to Kate, offering to pull her out of the saggy beanbag.

Kate's mouth twitched in a quick smile of delight. They couldn't think she was that strange, after all! She grabbed Izzy's hand and jumped up, wondering if it would be all right to suggest a couple of steps that she had learned in street dance, or if that would be pushing it a bit.

But then she remembered, and she felt the being sad fall down around her again. Her shoulders slumped. It was as if a thick black cloak had wrapped itself around her. People whose granddads had died didn't do dancing. Even if they wanted to, just a little bit. It didn't seem right to do fun things now.

She sat down again with a thump, and scrabbled for her book, staring down at it with blurry eyes.

"No," she said flatly. "Sorry. I can't." She set her face in a grim look, and made her voice very firm, to squash down the part of her that was saying, *Yes! Yes! I really want to join in!*

Izzy and Ella stared at her. "What do you mean, you can't?" Izzy demanded. "You wanted to, just a minute ago. Are you terrible at dancing or something?"

"Oh, just leave her!" Ella snapped. "She thinks she's so perfect. She's too important to hang around with us. Looking down her nose all the time. We didn't want you anyway," she added, turning to growl at Kate. "Go back to your book."

Kate gaped at her. She hadn't meant to be horrible at all. It was just that she couldn't join in now. . . It would be wrong. But she didn't want them to think she was stuck up.

"It isn't that I don't want to dance with you," she tried to explain, struggling up out of the beanbag again, and feeling stupid as she wobbled about. Izzy seemed to be trying not to laugh at her, and Ella just looked annoyed.

"You don't understand. . ." Kate stood there, gazing at them, and biting at her bottom lip. She couldn't explain about Granddad to two girls she'd never met before. She couldn't even talk to her mum or Molly about him without feeling awful. How could she explain it to these two?

"Well, explain it to us then!" Ella snapped, now completely out of patience. But Kate couldn't. The words were all stuck inside her, so instead she turned and ran out of the room to the coat racks.

Kate grabbed her rucksack and slid down the wall, so that she was sitting on the floor. Her legs felt wobbly. She even felt a bit sick. Hurriedly, she yanked at the zip on her rucksack, desperate to find Amos. But it was stuck, and she could feel the tears burning and prickling in the corners of her eyes. At last she managed to drag it open, and grab at Amos.

"What's the matter with you?"

Kate hadn't noticed, but someone had come up beside her. Izzy. Why had she followed her?

"Nothing!" Kate said sharply, stuffing Amos back into her bag, and glaring up at Izzy.

"I was only coming to see if you were OK!"

"Well, don't!" Kate yelled. "Just leave me alone!"

"You don't have to be like that. . ."

Kate watched miserably as Izzy retreated down the corridor. She was actually crying now too, and Kate felt awful. Being horrible to other people didn't make her feel better. But right now she didn't have the energy to be nice. Why couldn't she just stay at home on her own all day? In bed? Then she wouldn't have to talk to anybody.

She stood up wearily, and saw that Ella had been waiting for Izzy. She'd heard Kate shout. Izzy was still crying, and Ella was glaring up the corridor at Kate. She put her arm round Izzy's shoulders, and led her back into the classroom.

Kate sighed. So now they really, really hated her.

Ella's older brother was at the holiday club as well. Kate found that out at lunchtime, when she was sitting on her own, eating her sandwiches, and a boy walked past and tipped over her bottle of orange juice.

Kate jumped up, brushing uselessly at the juice all over the front of her jeans.

"Oh, sorry! It was an accident." The boy sounded apologetic, and when Jasmine hurried over to see what had happened, he pulled a tissue out of his pocket, and started patting at the juice puddled in Kate's lunch box. "I'm really sorry! I must have knocked the table or something. . ." He even looked sorry. Until Jasmine turned away to get some more paper towels and he smirked nastily at Kate.

"That's what you get for being horrible to my sister and her friend. Stupid stuck-up little baby."

Kate shook her head, staring at him. "But I wasn't! I mean, I did, but I wasn't meaning to be horrible. I just. . ." But how could she explain? She didn't want to tell this boy about Granddad either. She just shook her head again, feeling stupid.

"You think you're better than everyone else," he snapped back.

"No. . ."

Jasmine came back then, and the boy was all apologetic again. He fussed around, helping to clear up but "accidentally" sloshing more juice on to Kate, until Jasmine told him she'd do it and he could go back to his own lunch.

"Are you OK, Kate? Did the juice go on the rest of your lunch? I can get you something else to eat from the staffroom."

Kate shook her head. She wasn't hungry anyway. "It's all right," she murmured.

Jasmine went off to put away the mop, and Kate sat looking at her juice-spattered biscuits.

They were probably all right, wrapped up in their cling film, but she didn't open them. She zipped her lunch box shut again and put it in her rucksack, and then she just sat there, with her head hanging. Everyone was looking at her, she could tell. And whispering about her.

"She's crying. . ."

"Harry shouldn't have done that, it was mean."

"But didn't you hear? She was really horrible to Ella and Izzy."

"What did she do?"

"Oh, I don't know, but Ella said she was mean. Harry was just sticking up for Ella."

"She really is crying, look at her."

"She looks like she's wet herself, with that juice all over her jeans."

Then there was just giggling. Molly was over

there, somewhere, but she didn't stick up for Kate. She didn't say *anything*. Kate couldn't help thinking that Harry was horrible, but at least he looked after his sister.

Kate reached down, pretending to look for something in her bag, so she could touch Amos's fur. It was lucky that boy hadn't got juice on him too. He was right down at the bottom of her bag, and only a few drops had gone over the outside. The soft plush warmth of him tingled through her fingers, like the tiger purrs from last night, and she felt a little stronger. Brave enough to move.

Kate got up, tripping over chair legs and rucksacks, and once, she was almost sure, someone's stuck-out foot, as she hurried out of the room.

6

Kate spent the rest of the day skulking in and out of classrooms, avoiding Izzy and the others, and trying to stay within sight of one of the staff. She didn't want anything else spilled on her.

Actually, because she didn't want to get cornered by Harry and the others, she ended up having the best time she'd had at the holiday club so far. She stayed in the art room most of the afternoon, and did a massive painting of a tiger on a piece of cardboard. They had thick acrylic paints in there, the most amazing strong, rich colours. She'd been able to paint something that almost looked like her tiger, with amber eyes that glowed like jewels.

So she was feeling nearly happy, as she went to get her coat. She was a little late – she'd been helping to wash up the brushes and put things away. She was even looking forward to taking the painting home.

Kate shrugged her coat on, and unzipped her bag to whisper to Amos. "I left the painting to dry. I'll bring it home tomorrow." But as she reached down to the bottom of the bag, she found only her lunch box. No furry tiger.

Kate unzipped the other pockets, searching them frantically – even though she knew that the tiger wasn't in either of them.

Amos was gone.

Kate dropped the bag. She didn't know

what to do. She *needed* Amos. Desperately she dropped to her knees and searched again, throwing out her lunch box, and her jumper, her pencils, everything. But he still wasn't there.

"Kate, your mum's here. Are you ready?" Jasmine stood over her. "Have you lost something?"

Kate looked up at her, but she could hardly see. She couldn't talk, either. She could hardly *breathe*. Her shoulders heaved as she gasped and sobbed, trying to get words out. But she couldn't say it. *He's gone.*

"Oh, Kate!" Jasmine quickly picked up the things that Kate had scattered around, and stuffed them into her bag. "Come on. Let's go and find your mum and Molly."

She led Kate along the corridor with an arm

around her waist, which was good, because Kate couldn't actually see where she was going. Amos was her special present from Granddad, and now she had lost him. He was gone. If she didn't have the toy Amos, her real tiger wouldn't be there either. She would be completely alone. It was as if she'd been torn away from Granddad all over again.

"I'm really sorry, I've just found Kate by the coats, and she can't explain what's the matter. . ." Jasmine sounded worried. "She's had a much better day today, I don't know what's gone wrong. It's possible someone said something to her, about her granddad. Children can be cruel without meaning it sometimes. . ."

Kate felt her mum wrap her in a hug, and she slid her arms round Mum's waist. But she couldn't explain to Mum either. She couldn't answer any of the anxious questions Mum was pouring out.

"We'll take her home," Mum said at last, gently turning Kate round and leading her out to the car. Molly even opened the car door for her, and then she got in next to Kate instead of sitting in the front, and reached over to do her seatbelt, like Kate was tiny. It was nice.

"Mum, what's the matter with her?" Molly asked. Her voice was shaky, as though she was frightened, and Kate tried to look over at her. Molly was scared about her?

"I don't know, Moll. Kate, please, can you try to stop crying? Tell us what's wrong?" Mum was leaning round from the front, and she caught Kate's hand in hers. "Please, sweetheart?"

"I lost him. . ." Kate managed to force out. "Granddad. . ."

"Oh, Kate." And then, amazingly, Mum was crying too.

Kate stared at her. Mum never cried. She hadn't even cried in the hospital, when they'd gone to say goodbye, the day before Granddad died, or at the funeral. Kate had wondered about it, whether she wasn't all that sad. Mum had explained to them that Granddad was tired and ill and worn out, and it was better that he didn't come home and keep on feeling like that. Kate had thought that Mum believed it. That she was all right.

And now it was obvious that she wasn't. She was crying like Kate, just the same way, her shoulders shaking in huge, great gasps.

Kate managed to draw in a proper breath for the first time in ten minutes as she watched her mother uselessly pat a tissue against her face. "You do miss him then. . ." Kate murmured shakily. "You said it was for the best. . . You laughed, when Auntie Lyn was telling all those stories!"

"That doesn't mean I'm happy about it!" her mum almost howled, squeezing Kate's fingers as if she was frightened to let go.

Kate nodded, and reached out her other hand to grab on to Molly. "I didn't know. . ." she whispered. "I thought it was only me."

7

Mum sighed, and blew her nose. "I don't want to go home just yet," she murmured. "We'll go to the cafe."

"Granddad's cafe?" Kate sniffed, surprised. Granddad sometimes took her and Molly after school for a treat.

"Yes. I need some chocolate cake, what do you think?"

Mum sounded so different, Kate thought, as they drove through the centre of town to the little cafe, not far from their school. It was as though she'd been bottling everything up, and trying to go on just as before. And now she was actually admitting that she was sad.

"Chocolate cake was Granddad's favourite too," she said quietly.

Mum gave a little snort of laughter. "Maybe I inherited my love of chocolate cake from him," she suggested, as she parked down the road from the cafe. "Perhaps he'll be happy we're having it, and remembering him. He loved those little chocolate curls they put on the top. And the way it was too squidgy to pick up. He said a cake was only a proper cake if you needed a fork for it."

"We inherited it being our favourite from you," Kate agreed seriously. "Like the cats. I inherited loving cats from you too, and you got that from Granddad."

The cafe was tiny, but there were a few tables

free. Even Granddad's favourite table, just under the tiger. They always sat there if they could. The whole cafe was painted with a giant mural all the way round the walls inside. It made the room look like a wild, mad jungle, with huge trees and a river, and animals peering out all over the place. There were real plants in pots that sent out long leafy trails on wires across the ceiling too. Kate loved it. Every time they went she seemed to find a new creature. Some of them were really tiny, as though the artist had enjoyed setting a puzzle for the customers. Kate was almost sure that she and Molly were the only people who knew about the snails crawling along the top of the plug socket behind their table.

But as Molly hurried over to bag the tiger table, under the huge tiger snoozing on his tree branch, Kate hung back. The shock of seeing Mum cry had made her forget Amos, just for a few minutes. But that painted tiger looked so like him. So like the tiger who had snuggled up next to her in the shed.

And now she had lost him!

Her shoulders began to shake, and she pressed her hand across her mouth. She didn't want to make Mum cry again. It was almost scarier than crying herself.

"Katey-kitten. . . What is it? Here, come and sit down." Mum gently pushed her into a chair – but Kate was right underneath the tiger. She buried her face in her arms so she couldn't see him. What if she never found Amos? How would the real tiger come back without him?

Molly leaned down next to Kate and patted her arm. "Kate, where's your tiger?"

Kate couldn't answer her, but Molly had worked it out now, and she didn't give up. "You've been carrying him around with you all the time since – since Granddad went. You only put him down when Mum made you, for dinner, and baths. And you've kept him hidden in your bag for the holiday club." She pulled gently at Kate's hand, trying to see her face. "Kate, where is he?"

"They took him!" Kate gasped, looking up desperately at Molly. She was sure that it was true. Kate had been really horrible to Izzy. Even though she hadn't quite meant to be. And they must have taken Amos to teach her a lesson. Maybe it had been Harry too, Kate didn't know.

"Those girls, they were upset with me. I didn't really mean to be horrible, but I was. I just can't be friendly now, I'm too sad!"

"They took your tiger? That Granddad gave you?" Molly demanded angrily.

"Think so. . ." Kate sniffed.

"Is that why you were so upset when I picked you up?" her mum asked. "You'd just found that you hadn't got him?"

"He should have been in my rucksack," Kate whispered. "Under my lunch box. I didn't take him out, I know I didn't. Molly said I looked like a baby cuddling him. I didn't want anyone to laugh at me. I just kept him in there and went back and stroked him sometimes."

"Oh, Kate. . . You didn't really look babyish." Molly drew a pattern in some sugar that was spilled over the table. "I only said it because I was jealous. I wish I had something like your tiger, to remind me of Granddad."

Kate stared at her. "Really?"

"It's like you've got a special way to remember him," Molly added sadly. "You're lucky."

"But now he's gone," Kate gulped.

"We'll find him," Mum told her firmly. "I can explain to the leaders at the holiday club. We'll make sure you get him back."

Mum had promised. She even rang up the holiday club on her mobile, explaining what had happened, and asking them to look for Amos. She said if she had to she would make a huge fuss, until Kate had him back. But that didn't help right now. Kate still had to go to bed without him.

She sighed, and pulled the covers over her head, making a warm, muffled darkness.

If only a tiger could have exploded out of her rucksack that morning, and bitten Ella and Izzy in half. But it didn't seem to work like that. She only saw the tiger when she was on her own, and thinking about Granddad. Because Granddad had given her Amos, she supposed. He was hers and Granddad's together.

Kate pushed the duvet back a little and turned over, hunching it up around her shoulders. She was so tired, but she couldn't sleep now for worrying about tomorrow. And remembering all those whispery voices in the lunch room. She really didn't want to go back. Perhaps she could run away, she thought dreamily. She could run off to the forest reserve in India, and go and find the real Amos, the one they sent the money to.

She yawned, and closed her eyes, imagining walking through the trees and seeing him all at once. He'd come padding towards her, camouflaged among the shadows. Or perhaps he'd climb up out of the river. There had been a photo of one of the tigers swimming in the last letter from the tiger charity. He'd been shaking the water off his ears as he stepped on to the bank, all his whiskers splashy and dripping. She and Granddad had imagined swimming with tigers – holding on to their furry ruffs, and floating down a great river, looking up at the trees far above. And then climbing out and drying off on a furry tiger like a towel. Kate had said that a tiger's tail was the best way to dry between the toes. She smiled to herself. It could be true. She could swim with tigers. . .

In her dream, Kate hurried through the forest – a strange half-painted forest, like the cafe, partly real and partly flat. There were even tables here and there, hidden among the trees, and Kate could smell coffee, mixed in with the sweet, wet scent of leaves.

She was searching for Amos, of course. Not only her toy tiger but the real tiger he became. The tiger with big velvety paws who had wrapped her up tight and let her tears soak into his fur. He felt lost to her, the same way Granddad felt lost. But if she ran fast enough, she would catch him. He was just ahead of her, she was sure. There was a flash of dark orange fur, then it shimmered into the shadows again, the black stripes flickering away.

Kate raced through the forest, fighting her way through branches and creepers, her breath heaving. But always he was just too far ahead of her. Once she thought her outstretched fingers brushed his fur, but then he slipped away.

In the strange way of dreams, she suddenly understood that it wasn't real, moments before she was awake. Kate lay there twitching, panting, worn out just as she had been in the dream.

She reached out her hand to stroke the toy Amos, to make her feel better, but of course he wasn't there. Her fingers trailed uselessly across the bedclothes, and Kate gulped.

Then something nudged her hand – not the

silky plush fur of her toy tiger, but a rougher, warmer coat.

Kate cupped her fingers gently around the velvet of his muzzle, and felt his whiskers twitch against her hand, like thick wires.

"You're here!" she whispered in surprise. "I missed you. I thought I'd lost you. I didn't think you could ever come back."

She wriggled herself to the very edge of her bed, and draped her arm around his huge shoulders. She could just see him in the dark – a long, powerful shape stretched out on the spotty rug beside her bed. His amber eyes were glinting, and his striped black-tipped tail swished from side to side as she stroked him.

"Will you stay? Please?" Kate murmured sleepily. The tiger shifted beside her, and a deep, growly, loving voice answered her. The tiger sounded like Granddad, Kate thought, as her eyes flickered shut.

"I'll never leave you, Katey-kitten."

8

Kate woke up to thin streams of sunlight pouring between her bedroom curtains. The spotted fabric rippled gently in the breeze from the open window, and Kate could smell the freshness in the air. It was probably going to be a beautiful day. Except that she'd have to go back to the holiday club again.

She wrapped her arms around her knees, and frowned, thinking about the day before. Somehow, the idea of the holiday club didn't seem quite so bad this morning. Even though she didn't have Amos. And even though Ella and Izzy would be there again, giving her those sideways looks.

Because the tiger had come back.

He had been there, even without Amos to bring him. It was all right!

Kate lifted her head suddenly to look at the open window. Last night, he had come back, after her dream. He had been lying on her bedroom floor, next to the bed, purring in the darkness. He was probably longer than her bed was, Kate thought, grinning to herself. Not even counting his tail. He had come back to her – even though she didn't have the toy tiger any more. He had lain there with her, she had felt his fur and that had not been a dream, she was sure. Almost sure. She leaned over to look for hairs on the carpet, but she couldn't see any.

He must have gone back out of the window

again, to go hunting in the garden. He was probably out there now. Perhaps he was sleeping at the back of the flower bed. She could go downstairs and look, in a minute.

Or maybe she shouldn't. Perhaps it was cheating to look. She should just wait, and he would come, when she needed him. Then with the tiger curled around her, and his whiskers ticking her ears, it would be safe to remember.

"Kate!" Molly banged on her door, and then stuck her head around. "Mum's calling, didn't you hear? Breakfast."

Kate blinked at her. "All right."

Molly swung on the door handle and glanced at Kate, and then quickly away again as though she was nervous. "Are you OK?"

"Um. I think so. . ." Kate nodded slowly. It

was like getting up after you'd fallen over, and testing out if it hurt to walk. She was, mostly, all right. A bit battered. . .

"Well, you'd better hurry up. We've got to go to holiday club again, you know." That nervous look again. Then Molly added hurriedly, "You can stick with me and Erin, if you like."

Kate stared at her. "Thanks!" She smiled down at her knees. "I might for some of the time. But I want to do another painting." Maybe the tiger sleeping on a tree branch this time. Or coming towards her out of the river. With the splashing – maybe she could flick the paint off a toothbrush for the water droplets. She was actually looking forward to it, she decided, feeling surprised. "I'm coming!" she told Molly, scrambling out of bed.

"All right, well, I'm putting toast on for you, so hurry up." Molly had gone back to her bossy older sister voice, but Kate didn't mind. She pulled a cardigan on over her pyjamas, and followed Molly downstairs.

Mum was darting about the kitchen, making the packed lunches, and finding her work stuff at the same time. She looked distracted, but she stopped long enough to give Kate a hug, and kiss both her ears. "Eat some breakfast," was all she said, but Kate didn't mind. She took the plate of toast that Molly had handed her, and stood by the kitchen window. She wasn't really looking. . . But there might be a black-tipped tail wafting in those shadows where the long grass was.

Mum peered over Kate's shoulder, on her way to find the juice cartons. "Oh, look! Your lovely tulips, Kate! The ones you chose with Granddad." She caught her breath a little then, but she still sounded happy when she went on. "They're beautiful, those red and white stripes."

"Granddad was worried they might be a bit too bright," Kate murmured. "But I think he'd have liked them really."

Kate pulled out her old jeans, ones that wouldn't matter if she got paint on them, and sat down on her bed to put them on. Her curtains were still drawn, and they were flapping. She should shut the window, before they went out. But then the tiger might not be able to come in. . .

"Where are you now?" Kate whispered. "I won't come and look. I promise. Mum and Kate might see you, if I went and searched the garden. But – come back soon, won't you? Please?"

The soft hiss of her whispering echoed back to her across the room, making her blink and look up. Someone had answered her, in a whistling purr that deepened slowly into a roar. Someone was roaring in the garden. Actually, it sounded like someone was roaring just outside Kate's bedroom window.

He *was* there. He had come back for her! It was true, she didn't need the toy Amos after all. Kate leaned eagerly towards the window, waiting to hear the roar again.

Rrrrrrrrrrrrrrrrr. . .

"Is that you?" she asked, standing in front of the window, suddenly too nervous to pull the curtains open. A tiger couldn't fit on her windowsill – even though there was a dark shape, silhouetted against the early sun. But she could hear the purring roar. It sounded close. Someone was there.

Perhaps a small tiger? If he was curled up tight?

Kate inched the curtains apart, holding her breath and peering out.

Peering back at her hopefully was a huge, but far-too-thin, striped cat. He had broad shoulders, and his long back swung like a tiger's as he prowled up and down her windowsill. The sun was shining on his stripes – he was tawny-brown under them, not tiger-orange, but Kate thought he was as beautiful as any tiger.

"Was that you roaring?" Kate whispered

to him. "I thought you were a tiger."

The cat edged his face around her window, and eyed her solemnly. He had a great, shaggy head, with a golden tigery ruff and glowing amber eyes.

"Would you like to come in?" Kate asked, reaching out her fingers for him to sniff.

For such a big cat, he was very graceful, she thought admiringly as he stepped round through the window. His long, heavy black-tipped tail swirled around the glass, and he stood there looking at her.

Kate remembered a tail just like that, swishing back and forth on her rug. Could it have been a long, brown and black, striped tabby tail? And not a tiger's, after all?

"Was it you last night?" Kate murmured,

running her hand down his long back. He was thinner than he should be, she could tell – the bony lumps on his back stood out. "What happened to you?" she wondered. "Are you a stray?" Then she caught her breath hopefully. "Do you need someone to look after you?" She stepped away from the window and sat down on the end of her bed, eyeing the cat sideways, hoping he'd be brave enough to follow her in.

The cat looked at the bed as if he already knew how comfortable it might be for sleeping on, as if he had been here before, and then he jumped after her, landing with a thump. He padded at the rumpled covers, and seemed to approve. Then he set off and marched around her, lifting his paws up high, and all the time purring and purring.

Kate looked at his velvety paws and smiled. "You're my tiger... Was it you all the time? Even in the shed that first night?"

The cat purred loudly again, and butted the top of his head against Kate's cheek. A tawny, gingery hair floated on to the windowsill, and Kate felt laughter bubbling inside her. Laughter, and just a hint of disappointment. Granddad hadn't sent her a tiger guardian – and Amos wasn't anything more than her favourite, most treasured toy. There hadn't been a tiger who had wrapped himself around her.

But this cat had still kept her from missing Granddad. He had been there when she needed him. And the cat *had* come because of Granddad, Kate was sure. The brown tabby had smelled the packet of treats that Granddad kept up on the shelf in the shed. He'd come sniffing for cat treats, and found a girl instead, a girl who needed something to hold on to. He'd curled up with her, and given her a way to remember.

Kate laughed. "Oh, if only Granddad could have seen you." She stopped for a moment, and took a deep breath, but it was all right. It was good to talk about Granddad. "You'd have been just the sort of cat he'd like," she went on determinedly. "He loved big cats, and stripy ones were his favourite. He'd have given you all his cat treats. I'll go and get them for you in a minute, out of the shed."

The cat stopped circling and stared up at her with golden-amber eyes. He had enormously hairy ears, Kate noticed, just like Granddad, and the tiger. And the same white whiskery eyebrows. But he was himself, and that was all. That was quite enough.

Look out for more by
HOLLY WEBB

A
Cat Called
PENGUIN

HOLLY WEBB

Illustrated by Polly Dunbar

Everyone thinks Penguin is a silly name for
a cat, but Alfie thinks it's perfect. To Alfie,
he's the best cat in the world.

Penguin loves to play in the overgrown garden
next door. But when a new girl moves in and
reclaims it, Alfie worries she might think
Penguin belongs to her too!

What's living in Ben and Cassie's garden?

There are strange rustlings coming from the greenhouse, and something has eaten all of the sausage rolls they left out. It could be a bear. . . Everyone knows that bears love sausage rolls.

Can Ben and Cassie catch it? Or at least see it for real? They're definitely going to try.

Turn over for a sneak peek of

The CHOCOLATE Dog

Amy wriggled. Choc had his nose in her ear again. "Ow, Choccie, don't." She leaned away from him, giggling. "It's cold." They'd been in the car for ages, four hours at least, and the heat was making Choc's chilly nose feel icy. He'd been licking the bare part of her shoulder or sticking his nose in her ear every few minutes since they'd left the house.

Choc hated being stuck in his dog crate in the boot of the car. He saw no reason why he couldn't sit next to Amy and Lara in the back seat. He knew that was where he was meant to be – right in the middle of the two girls, so they could both make a big fuss of him. He stared through the wire of the crate with mournful chocolate-brown eyes, and slobbered down the back of Amy's vest top.

"Uurgh, Choc. . ." Amy squashed sideways so he couldn't dribble on her neck any more, and peered through the wire at him. "I know you're bored, but *please* stop licking me. . ."

Choc's eyes were round and soulful like Maltesers now, and Amy smiled. She could never resist that look. She pushed two fingers through the wire of the crate and scratched him behind the ears. He sighed with delight, leaning his head up against the side, eyes closed, shivering happily. Behind the ears was the best place. A really good behind-the-ears scratch could have him on the floor with all four paws in the air. He slumped gradually down to the floor with a long sigh.

Amy eased her hand back from the crate. Choc had fallen asleep, she thought, blinking as the air in the car slanted suddenly green. The trees were arching over the road, pushing against each other so close that the car was driving through a green tunnel, a tunnel with strange dappled patterns of sunlight here and there. Amy wondered if anyone else had noticed. Dad was only looking straight ahead. That was probably a good thing, if you were driving, Amy thought sleepily. It was the middle of the afternoon, and it felt like they'd been driving all day. Her little sister, Lara, looked like she was about to melt into her pink car seat, and their mum was fanning herself with a paper fan Amy had made her at school.

Amy leaned her head against the car window and sighed. She was hot, and half-asleep like

Choc, and the car seat was sticking to her legs. She took a breath, about to ask Mum if they were nearly there, and then caught Dad's eye in the mirror, and didn't. Everyone was grumpy, and Mum had been grumpy all week. The baby wasn't due for another month, but Amy was already feeling fed up with it, and the way it was making Mum so tired and cross.

Lara did it instead. "Mum, are we there yet?"

"No." Mum's voice was tight and tired. She shifted uncomfortably in her seat, as though she was just as sticky as Amy. And about four times the size. She was enormous.

"If we were there we'd be able to see the sea, Lara, wouldn't we?" Mum sighed.

"Not if there was something in the way," Lara muttered. "Like a wall. Or trees. Houses."

"Lara, don't," Dad said firmly. "Ten more minutes."

"That's what you said last time," Amy couldn't help putting in. Dad seemed to think they wouldn't notice. He'd been saying ten more minutes for ages. "Oh! Did you see? That was a sign for Sandmouth! Five, it said, five miles."

"There you are, then. Ten minutes," Dad agreed smugly. "Like I said."

"It's pink!" Amy stared at the cottage as they pulled up outside.

Her mother nodded, a little doubtfully. "When they said it was called Shrimp Cottage, I didn't realize it would be painted shrimp pink. It's a bit bright. . ."

Amy smiled. "I like it." The cottage was the

same colour as pink candy shrimps, the ones on the penny sweets shelf at the sweetshop they went to after school sometimes. She loved those. She always had to save one for Choc, though, otherwise he knew she'd had them – he had a nose like a sniffer dog. If she didn't give him a shrimp, he'd sit there and howl at her until she said she was sorry.

Amy had to be very careful what she fed him. Choc didn't only have eyes like Maltesers, he'd happily wolf down half a packet of them too, and dogs weren't supposed to have chocolate; it was really bad for their insides. Choc just didn't seem to think so. Amy could understand why – after all, they *had* named him Chocolate, so why couldn't he eat it?

Mum and Amy and Lara had made an

emergency appointment at the vet's last Christmas, after they'd come down in the morning and found that Choc had eaten all the chocolate Christmas decorations. And the foil, unless he'd carefully taken it off and binned it. He must have climbed on the arm of the sofa to reach the top ones, Amy reckoned.

The vet had said he thought Choc would be fine, he'd probably just be really sick, because milk chocolate wasn't as bad as the dark kind. But Choc hadn't even burped. He came home from the vet's sulking like he always did (he would duck right down in the car and try to dig his claws into the floor of his car crate if they even drove past). Then when they got in the house, he whisked past Mum, who was trying to head him off into the kitchen – she would rather he was sick on a tiled floor – and back into the living room to see if the tree had grown any more chocolate. It hadn't, so he had a peppermint candy cane instead.

Choc was whining in his car crate now. He knew they'd stopped, and he couldn't stand being shut up in the boot for much longer.

"We'd better get him out." Dad took his seat belt off and stretched wearily. "Poor dog sounds as though he's got his legs crossed. Why don't you girls take him for a quick run round that patch of grass over there? He can have a proper walk later, once we've unpacked. I need to go and pick up the keys from the cottage next door."

"Can't we go to the beach?" Amy asked hopefully, but Dad was already making for the next-door cottage.

The beach was so close – just down a long

flight of stone steps on the other side of the road. Amy could hear the sea, and see it. It was almost blue. Not blue like on a postcard, where the sea was a shiny jewel colour. More of a greenish, brownish, blueish thing, heaving up and down like a blanket someone was shaking. She wanted to go and stand at the edge of it. Dip her toes in it. And she could tell Choc wanted to do the same. His ears were blowing in the sea-smelling breeze, and he kept looking up at her hopefully. Every time they went to the park, he tried to jump in the duck pond, and this was the biggest duck pond he'd ever seen. Amy crouched down next to him. "It doesn't have enormous ducks to match," she murmured, running her fingers down the curls of his ears. "But there might be fish, I suppose," she added doubtfully. "Oh, and seagulls. But they look mean. I'd leave them alone."

Choc quivered with excitement. He was quite well trained – Dad had taken him to classes – so he stayed sitting, but he was sitting and leaning forward about as much as he possibly could without falling over. His nose was stretched out towards those steps. It didn't help that Lara was dancing up and down on the edge of the pavement, trying to get a better view of the sea. Her little sister wasn't as well trained as Choc, Amy thought, grinning to herself. She needed a lead more than he did.

Dad was coming back now, clutching a set of keys and a folder. Mum had been leaning against the front of the car, having a drink of water, but now she turned to look out at the sea. "Isn't it lovely?" she murmured. "We'll go down for a walk later, you two. Let's just get settled in first."

As Dad unlocked the door, the two girls raced in. There was something fascinating about the cottage – just because it was so different to home. Their house was like all the others in the street, a semi, painted white, with a square of garden at the front and a long thin strip at the back. Over the fence at the end of their back garden was another garden, and a whole street that mirrored theirs. If Amy went to tea with a friend who lived anywhere near, she pretty much knew where all the rooms were without asking. Although sometimes the stairs were on the wrong side of the hallway, which just looked weird.

Here, it was different. Shrimp Cottage was squashed up between two other houses, and neither of them matched. Inside, it opened up a little, somehow getting wider at the back, like a little burrow. Tunnels opened out here and there. The girls ran into a living room with fat, sagging sofas and a small stove in the fireplace, then a kitchen with a long wooden table, and last, a little glass sunroom full of wicker chairs, and one huge spider plant that seemed to be trying to take over the world.

A twisting wooden staircase led up to the bedrooms. A huge one for their parents, with a great big bed – Mum would be pleased. She said she needed a bed and a half now. Then there was a pretty blue-and-white room with striped wallpaper and fussy patchwork bedcovers.

"You can have this one," Amy said quickly to Lara, even though there was a view of the sea. It looked wonderful from the high window, much bluer somehow, with late afternoon sun streaming golden across it. She loved the wide window sill too. But perhaps the other room would have an even better view, and this one was just too frilly.

Mum had struggled up the stairs behind them with an armful of Lara's soft toys. "There's only one room, girls. We did say, don't you remember? We booked late; with the baby, everything was a bit disorganized. I wasn't sure I was up to going away, and then there weren't many places that would take Choc as well. The cottage *is* a bit small, but we'll manage."

Amy gaped at her. "One room? You mean I have to share with Lara?"

"I'm having this bed!" Lara bounced on to the bed by the window, seizing her mermaid doll from Mum. She sat cross-legged on the bed, clutching the doll and smirking at Amy.

"But Mum. . ." Amy gulped. She remembered now, but it hadn't seemed to matter that much a few weeks before. She'd been so excited about going on holiday that she'd forgotten it meant a whole week in the same bedroom as Lara. "She talks in her sleep!"

Her mum sighed and eased herself down on to the other bed. Amy's bed. "I know. But not very often."

"And she sleepwalks." Amy slumped down next to Mum on the bed. Her bed now. "I'll wake up and she'll be standing next to me looking all spooky. It makes me go shivery when she does that!"

Lara sniggered and made a ghostly, toothy face at Amy.

Amy lay backwards, gazing up at the ceiling. She could hear paws scrabbling on the wooden stairs – Choc was coming to see where they'd got to.

Choc peered whiskerily round the bedroom door and flapped his ears happily at Amy and Lara.

Amy laughed. He had his red fleece blanket in his teeth, the one that usually lined his basket at home. It had been in the dog crate with him, to make him feel better about the journey. Now he gazed lovingly at Amy's mum, doing his best big-eyed look. The one that said *You know I am clean, loving and perfectly house-trained. . .*

"Where's Choc sleeping?" Amy asked thoughtfully.

"In the kitchen, like he does at home."

Her mum sounded surprised.

"Couldn't he sleep up here with us? As a holiday treat?" She turned over, squinting hopefully up at Mum. She'd tried asking for Choc in her room before, but Mum hadn't liked the idea. If it was just for the holidays, though. . . She'd rather share a room with Choc than Lara, any day. But she'd settle for both.

Lara bounced up and down on her bed excitedly. "Yes, yes! Please, Mum!"

Choc danced over to her, dropping his blanket and licking her bare toes lovingly.

Lara pulled her feet back up on to the bed with a squealing giggle, and Amy laughed too.

"Well, I suppose. . ." her mum started to say, smiling at them all, and Amy hugged her. (Carefully.)

"Yes! Thanks, Mum!"

"I want him on my bed!" Lara crouched down next to Choc, and he licked her ear.

"He can choose," Amy said hurriedly. She didn't want Mum changing her mind because they were squabbling.

"Girls, you do realize. . ." Mum trailed off, and then started getting up, as if she'd changed her mind about what she was going to say.

"What?" Amy bounced up to help pull. "What is it?"

"Thank you, sweetheart." Mum looked down

at her worriedly. "When the new baby comes – it'll need somewhere to sleep."

"Won't the baby go in your room? In the Moses basket?" Amy asked slowly.

"Maybe for the first few weeks," her mum agreed. "But we need to get the room ready. Put the cot somewhere."

Lara looked up at her and frowned. "Somewhere where?"

"The smallest room. Your room, Lara," Mum said gently. "Amy's room is really big. There's room for both of you."

"There isn't!" Amy shook her head, her eyes panicky. There just wasn't!

Her lovely bedroom. Full of Lara. How was there going to be any room left for her?

HOLLY has always loved animals. As a child, she had two dogs, a cat, and at one point, nine gerbils (an accident). Holly's other love is books. Holly now lives in Reading with her husband, three sons and a very spoilt cat.